PUFFIN BOOKS

THE LITTLE LIGHTHOUSE KEEPER

Ray, the little lighthouse keeper, lives in a red and white striped lighthouse which stands on a big black rock in the middle of the sea. Ray and his furry, fat dog, Croup, have all sorts of seaworthy adventures. They save a fog-bound ship, rescue a little bird, get a special message in a bottle and celebrate Ray's birthday!

Margaret Joy has written many books for children. She is also a full-time teacher and lives in North Wales, where her husband is the headmaster of a school for deaf children. They have four children.

Other books by Margaret Joy

The Little Lighthouse Keeper

Margaret Joy
Illustrated by Toni Goffe

Puffin Books

PUFFIN BOOKS

Published by the Penguin Group
Penguin Books Ltd, 27 Wrights Lane, London W8 5TZ, England
Viking Penguin, a division of Penguin Books USA Inc.
375 Hudson Street, New York, New York 10014, USA
Penguin Books Australia Ltd, Ringwood, Victoria, Australia
Penguin Books Canada Ltd, 2801 John Street, Markham, Ontario, Canada L3R 1B4
Penguin Books (NZ) Ltd 182–190 Wairau Road, Auckland 10, New Zealand

Penguin Books Ltd, Registered Offices: Harmondsworth, Middlesex, England

First published by Viking Kestrel 1988
Published in Puffin Books 1989
10 9 8 7 6 5 4 3

Printed in England by Clays Ltd, St Ives plc
Filmset in Times

Contents

Contents

Croup,
the Sea-dog

ON a big black rock in the middle of the sea stood a red-and-white striped lighthouse. This was the home of the little lighthouse keeper, Ray.

At first, Ray had wanted to be a sailor, but whenever he went to sea, he was seasick. So then he got the job of lighthouse keeper on the big

black rock, and he had been there ever since.

He was never lonely. Seabirds came to rest on the rock. Seals clambered up on to it to sunbathe. Puffins and gannets dived off it for fish.

And, of course, there was his dog, Croup.

Croup was fat and furry, and followed Ray everywhere. Ray first called him Croup after hearing him bark. (If you say "croup" out loud, rather gruffly, you'll know exactly how he sounded – just like someone with a bad cough.)

"Come on, Croup," said Ray every morning. "Time to see to the Light."

One morning Ray set off up the ninety-six spiral stairs which led to the very top of the lighthouse. Croup followed him with a little jerky jump up each stair. They were both puffing a little when they reached the

top. Here was the Light Room, where the huge Light shone all night long. It warned ships to keep well away from the big black rock that stuck up sharply

out of the sea. Ray inspected
the Light.

"Seems all ship-shape." He
nodded.

Then he polished the
windows which went all round
the Light Room.

12

"Bit of a mist over the water today," he said to Croup. "Hope we're not going to have one of those foggy spells. Ah, well, if we do, I'll have to switch on the fog horn. We don't want any ships crashing on to the black rock in the dark."

Ray went down the spiral stairs, and Croup lolloped after him, a step at a time. They reached the ground and walked outside. Ray looked out across the water.

"It's very still today," he said. "I don't like it. I can't even hear the seabirds. And the mist is getting thicker."

13

"Croup, croup," barked Croup, and the echo went all round the lighthouse.

Ray shivered. "I don't like mist at all," he said. "And sailors don't like it either. They

14

hate sailing in fog when they can't see a thing."

By evening the fog was really thick. Ray and Croup stood at the door of the lighthouse. Everything was very still. They could hear the faint swish of the sea, but they couldn't see it. There was nothing but whiteness all around.

Ray switched on the Light and the fog horn. A great beam of light shone into the whiteness. The fog horn started to sound. (If you sing "Durr . . . durr" aloud, then count to six in your head and sing "Durr . . . durr" again, you'll know

LIGHT HORN (FOG)

exactly what it sounded like.)

Ray and Croup ate their supper.

"I hope those ships out there can hear our fog horn," said Ray.

Croup didn't answer. He was eating his favourite meaty snacks.

16

Suddenly Ray said, "Hey!
Did you hear that?"

Croup looked up.

"The fog horn's stopped,"
cried Ray. "I'll have to try and

mend it. But how can we warn ships off the rock? They'll never see the light in this fog."

"Croup, croup," barked Croup anxiously.

"Yes, yes," said Ray, "you've got a lovely loud bark, old fellow. They'd be able to hear you all right. They'd hear you miles away."

"Croup, croup!" barked Croup again, as loudly as he could.

Ray looked at his furry fat friend again – and suddenly realized what he was saying. "Ah, yes, old fellow, you *have* got a good strong bark. They certainly *would* hear you miles away. Do you think you could keep barking while I mend the fog horn?"

Croup answered with a wag of his tail and made for the door. Ray opened it for him. Croup went out into the fog and sat at the edge of the rock.

Ray wrapped a thick rug round him. "Stay there then, old fellow," he said. "I'm off to mend the fog horn."

"Croup . . . croup," barked Croup into the whiteness. He counted up to six in his head, then barked again, "Croup . . . croup." It sounded just like someone with a bad cough, and it echoed out into the thick fog.

Not very far off, a ship was sailing very slowly through the fog. There was whiteness all around. The captain looked at his chart.

"Somewhere near here," he said, "there's a big rock with a lighthouse on it. I hope we don't crash into it. We can't see a thing in this fog."

"Can't hear anything either," said the mate.

They both strained their ears. Suddenly the captain heard a faint sound, then another. "Did you cough?" he asked the mate.

"Cough, sir? No, sir," said the mate, looking puzzled.

They strained their ears again. There was another faint sound, followed by another.

"Did you cough, sir?" asked the mate.

"Me, mate?" said the captain. "No, mate."

They both listened again.

"It's someone coughing," said the mate.

"Must be on the big rock,"

said the captain. "We must be very near it."

"We'd better stop sailing then," said the mate.

"We'll drop anchor here," said the captain. "We can stay here safely until morning light."

The mate nodded. "Perhaps the fog will have cleared by then."

"There it goes again," said the captain. "It's a terrible cough."

"Good thing we heard it in time," said the mate.

They lowered the anchor and went to sleep in their bunks.

When the sun came up the next morning, the fog had cleared. The sky was blue and gold, and the sea was silver.

"There's the lighthouse rock, just over there," shouted the captain, coming up on deck. "Good thing we didn't sail any nearer."

"We might have had a dreadful crash," agreed the mate.

"I can still hear that coughing sound," said the captain.

"But it's very faint now," the mate replied.

"It's coming from the rock," said the captain. "From that red

thing on the rock." He looked
through his binoculars. "Well,
bless my barnacles," he cried.
"It's a dog wrapped in a red
rug! Here, take a look, mate!"

At that moment the real fog
horn boomed out across the
sea: "Durr . . . durr." Ray had
mended it at last. He raced
down the spiral stairs and out
on to the rock.

26

There sat fat little Croup, just where he had left him. He was very cold, and his voice had nearly gone. Ray picked him up and carried him back inside. Soon Ray had a roaring fire going, and Croup was sitting in

front of it, crunching a bowl of meaty snacks.

"Yum, yum," he thought. "This is better than sitting on a flat rock with a cold bot all night."

"I'll put a drop of rum in your water bowl," said Ray. "You're a real sea-dog, old fellow, a real sea-dog."

"Croup," whispered Croup happily, and thumped his tail on the floor.

The Zit Zit Bird

One day, when the sea was very calm, the little lighthouse keeper, Ray, sat fishing at the water's edge. His dog, Croup, was swimming nearby.

"Come and play with me," he barked at the fish. He tried to catch them in his paws, but they always wriggled away. He climbed out on to the rock and

shook himself. A shower of drops sprayed over Ray.

"Hey, watch out, Croup!" he cried.

Croup lolloped off across the rocks. "Come and play with me," he barked at the seagulls.

But they flew up in the air, screeching, when they saw him coming.

Croup went over to a rock pool. "Play with me," he barked at a crab. But it ran into a crack in a rock.

Suddenly Croup saw something. He barked for Ray to come and look. The little lighthouse keeper put down his fishing rod and went over to Croup. He was sniffing at a sticky brown thing lying on the rock.

Ray bent down over it. "It's a seabird," he said. "It's a little tern – and she's covered in oil.

It must be from an oil tanker.
Poor little bird."

The little tern opened her
eyes and looked at Ray. She
opened and shut her beak, but
no sound came out. Then she

tried to move her wings, but they were sticky with oil.

"Will you play with me?" barked Croup. He licked the little tern, but the oil was too sticky to lick off, and it tasted nasty too.

"Poor little bird," said Ray again. "Let's take her into the house."

He carried the little tern to the lighthouse. Croup followed close behind, sniffing. He could smell the thick black oil on the bird.

Ray laid the little tern on a blanket in front of the fire. Then he fetched some old rags, a

bowl of warm water and a
bottle of detergent.

"This will get it off," he said.

Croup watched as Ray
carefully wiped the little tern's
feathers again and again. The
black oil came off on the rags.
It smelt horrible. Croup

sneezed. The little tern opened her eyes and blinked. She opened and shut her beak, but still no sound came out. Ray wiped her with more warm water and more detergent. Slowly more black oil came away on the rags.

"She's nearly clean," said Ray.

Now they could see that her feathers were grey and white and her head was black. Her beak and legs were bright yellow. Croup came closer and licked the little tern again.

"Croup, croup?" he asked softly. "Will you play with me?"

The little tern opened her
beak and said, "Zit, zit, zit . . ."
Her eyes were brighter now,
and she was trying to flutter her
wings.

"They're still a bit sticky,"
said Ray. "Just a little more

detergent and a little more wiping, then you'll be almost clean, little tern."

She struggled to get to her feet. Ray gave her some scraps

of raw fish. She pecked at them, then – gulp – she had eaten them all. She dipped her beak into the water he brought and drank in gulps. Then she fluttered her wings. Ray sat back and watched, and so did Croup.

She flew from the floor to the chair. She flew from the chair up on to the table. She flew from the table up on to the cupboard.

"She's ready to go back to sea," said Ray.

He opened the lighthouse door, and the little tern flew out into the sunlight. Croup watched her beat her wings and fly to the edge of the black rock.

She swooped away over the
water to the other birds.

"Now she'll never play with
me," thought Croup sadly.

He stood with the little
lighthouse keeper, watching the
flocks of seabirds out at sea.
Suddenly something came
speeding towards them.

40

"Look out," cried Ray, "she's come back!"

The little tern stopped in mid-air and dropped a shining fish in front of them. "Zit, zit, zit," she cried to them, then beat her wings and swooped off again.

"I think she was saying,

41

'Thank you'," said Ray. "Come on, Croup, let's go and cook this for tea."

Every day after that, the little tern flew down to visit the lighthouse keeper and his furry fat dog. Croup was always pleased to see her and barked.

Then the little tern pretended to be frightened and fluttered her wings and dive-bombed him. Sometimes she balanced on Croup's head and let him give her a ride. Sometimes she flew away to the waves and skimmed across their white tops; then she would come back with a fish in her beak and drop it in front of them. Sometimes she landed on Ray's shoulder and would sit there, softly saying, "Zit, zit, zit . . ."

One day Ray gently put a ring round her leg with the name of the lighthouse written on it.

"Now if she gets lost or injured," he said to Croup, "people will know where her home is, and let me know."

Then, one morning, Ray decided to go fishing. He took his fishing rod and went out. His furry fat dog followed him

across the rocks; they were cold
and slippery. Suddenly, Ray's
foot skidded, and he fell down.

"Ouch!" he yelled. "My
ankle! I can't move . . . Oh,
Croup, oh, it hurts."

He shut his eyes. He had
gone very pale. Croup licked

45

his hands, but he didn't move.
Croup lolloped back to the
lighthouse and dragged out the

red rug. He pulled it over Ray
to keep him warm. Then he
started to bark for help:
"Croup! Croup! Croup!"

But no one else lived on the
big rock except the seals – and
they took no notice. And there
were no ships passing by. But
the birds heard him, and they
told one another.

In a few minutes Croup
heard, "Zit? zit?" The little tern
came swooping down. She
landed next to Ray. She peered
at him with her bright eyes,
then she looked at Croup. She
flew close to him and rubbed
her head against his front paw,

47

as if to say, "Don't worry, I'll
see to it." Then she took off,
beating her wings strongly. She
flew low over the waves towards
the mainland.

Croup looked at Ray again.
He was groaning. "Oh, my

ankle," he gasped. "I don't think I can walk on it. I'd better stay here until it feels a bit stronger, old fellow."

Croup licked his cheek and sat on guard beside him. He watched the sky for a sign of the little tern coming back.

After quite a time he heard a boat, a motor-boat. It was cutting through the water. It stopped at the edge of the black rock. It was their friend, Luke, the coastguard, from the mainland. He got out of his boat and tied it up to the metal ring in the rock.

"Ahoy, there!" he called.

"Anyone at home?"

Croup stood up and barked as loud as he could. "Croup! Croup! Croup!"

"Hello, Croup," called Luke, coming across the rock, "hello,

old fellow."

Then he saw Ray and bent to look at his ankle.

"So this is the trouble," he said. "A little tern came knocking on my window. She wouldn't stop. So I went outside and she kept dive-bombing me. She seemed to want me to do something. Then she sat on my

shoulder and I spotted the ring on her leg. She let me take it off – and there was your address. So I thought I'd better come over and see if you needed help."

At this moment the little tern swooped down over them.

"There she is again – what a clever little thing she is," Luke said.

Ray nodded. "Well, Croup and I rescued her when she was covered with oil. I think she wants to repay us now." He smiled. "And one good turn deserves another, you know."

Message in a Bottle

Ray was having a busy day.
First, he polished the windows
of the Light Room. Then he did
his washing and hung it out to
dry. (There's always a sea
breeze round a lighthouse.)
Then he took a dustpan and
brush and brushed the dust off
all the spiral stairs.

"Croup, croo-oo-oo-oup!"

choked Croup, as the dust got
in his nose and mouth.

"Well, go outside then, silly,"
said Ray. "I'll be with you in a
minute. I'm coming out to do
some painting."

55

He tipped the stair-dust into the dustbin and went outside with two pots of paint, one red and one white, and two brushes.

He started work at the foot of the lighthouse, and began to paint it white. Swish-swosh, went the brush, swish-swosh. The wet paint shone in the sunshine. Croup followed after him, wiping splashes off the ground with a rag under his paw. The little tern flew to and fro near the shining paint. If she saw a patch that Ray had forgotten to paint, she flapped her wings near it, calling, "Zit, zit – missed it. Zit, zit – missed it."

Ray finished painting all round the foot of the lighthouse with white paint. Then he started painting further up with red paint. But the sun had gone in; grey clouds were blowing

across the sea; spots of rain were beginning to fall; the waves were getting higher.

"There's going to be a storm!" shouted Ray.

He quickly took the painting things inside and ran out again to fetch in his washing.

"Come on, little tern. Come on, Croup. Indoors, quick!"

They all went in out of the strong wind. Ray shut the doors and windows tight. Now the wind was howling round the lighthouse. Waves were smacking into the black rock and sending spray shooting up into the air.

But inside it was quiet. The fire was warm. Croup lay down in front of it on his red rug, with his nose on his paws. The little tern went to sleep on the back of an armchair. Ray sat at the table.

In front of him were bits of
wood he had found washed up
on the rock. He took out a
sharp little knife and began to
carve one of the bits of wood
into a ship. He carved the sides
and the deck and the masts.
Then he made little paper sails

and stuck them on to the masts.

Usually, when the little sailing ships were finished, Ray painted them bright colours. He made the masts lie flat, and pushed each little ship inside a bottle. Then he poked a long stick inside the bottle and made

the masts stand up in the air
again, so that the sails were
spread out. It looked as though
the ship was sailing along inside
the bottle. Then Ray pushed

the cork back in the neck of the bottle. He loved to make the little sailing ships for his family and friends.

"I've made one for Cousin Tim, and one for Tom, and one for Tubby," he thought. "And now I'm going to paint this little ship blue and silver for Auntie Milly – but I haven't got an empty bottle to put it in."

He went to look in his cupboard, but the only bottle in there was full of rum, so that was no good. But he had a little swig while he was there, and then went back to the table, singing. This is what he sang:

"A little drop of rum
Warms your tum, warms your
tum!"

Then he climbed all the
ninety-six spiral stairs to make
sure the Light was shining
brightly through the storm.

The bad weather lashed the
lighthouse for two whole days.
On the third morning
everything was still. The sun
was warm again. The sea was
as smooth as glass. Ray and
Croup went for a walk round
the rock.

"Croup, croup," said the
furry fat dog, barking at

something floating nearby. It was a large bottle.

"Ahoy, there," said Ray. "Just what I'm after."

Croup lolloped down to the water's edge and pulled the bottle ashore with his paw.

Ray picked it up. "There's a piece of paper inside," he said.

He pulled out the cork and then carefully eased out the piece of paper. Croup stood looking up at Ray, and the little tern came to perch on his shoulder. They both wanted to know what it was all about.

"Why, it's floated across from the coastguard station," said Ray. "It's from Luke. This is what he says:

Dear Everybody,
    Wasn't that a dreadful
    storm? Hope you are all
    right. Here's a riddle to

cheer you up.
What lies on the sea-bed and
shivers? A nervous wreck."

"Hee, hee, hee," chuckled
Ray.
"Zit, zitty-zit, zit," twittered
the little tern and nearly fell off
Ray's shoulder.

"Croup, croupy-croup, croup," gruffawed Croup, and rolled over and over laughing until he fell into a rock pool.

"Good old Luke," said Ray. "He's certainly cheered us up – and, as well as that, he's sent me just what I needed to finish off Auntie Milly's ship-in-a-bottle."

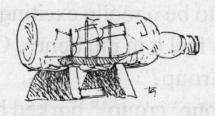

Birthday Surprises

The little lighthouse keeper jumped out of bed.

"It's my birthday!" he cried. "The sun is shining and it's going to be a really exciting day – I can feel it in my bones. Can't you, Croup?"

"Croup, croup!" barked his furry fat dog. He ran to find Ray's shoes and polished each

one with the furry part of his
paws.

"Oh me, oh my, Croup!" said
Ray. "Shiny shoes for my
birthday – thanks, old fellow."

71

"Croup!" said the furry fat dog, and thumped his tail on the floor.

Just then, the little tern shot in through the window. She landed on Ray's shoulder and

dropped a fish on to the bed.

"Oh me, oh my, little tern!" said Ray. "A fish for my birthday – thanks, old girl."

"Zit, zit," said the little tern softly, rubbing her head against his ear. Then she flew out again.

Ray climbed the spiral stairs. Croup followed him with a little jerky jump up each stair. They inspected the Light, and Ray polished the windows.

"There," he said, "that's done. Now I can do just what I like today: it's my birthday. It's going to be a really exciting day – I can feel it in my bones."

73

He ran down the spiral stairs and Croup lolloped after him. They shared the fish for breakfast and drank lots of strong tea (Ray's was in a cup and Croup's was in a saucer).

Ray carried a deckchair outside and sat in the sun. He tied knots in the corners of his hanky and put it on his head for a sun hat. Then he shut his eyes. Then he yawned. Then he fell asleep. Croup lay with his nose on his paws and slept too . . .

After a long time, Ray blinked and woke up. He stretched and yawned.

"This isn't very exciting," he said sadly. "I thought my birthday was going to be great – I thought I felt it in my bones."

Just then, Croup's ears pricked up. They both heard the sound of a motor-boat. Ray looked through his binoculars.

"It's Luke," he said. "Good old Luke. He knows it's my birthday, and he's come to wish me many happy returns of the day."

He looked through his binoculars again.

"Oh," he said, "there's a great big box in the boat. It must be a birthday present. Perhaps it's from Auntie Milly, or from Cousin Tim, or Tom, or Tubby. Perhaps they've *all* put presents in the box – or perhaps there's one giant present from all of them! Oh, I am excited! What can it be?"

He ran across to the edge of
the big rock.

"Ahoy there, Ray," called
Coastguard Luke.

He tied his motor-boat to the
ring in the rock. Then he lifted

the big box out of his boat.

"This is for you," he said.

"Oh me, oh my!" said Ray.
"I love opening parcels!
Whatever can it be? Ooh, I am
excited."

He pulled off the string and
ripped open the box. Then he

stopped and stared. "What's this?" he asked. "Dusters? Old rags? A sponge? Polish?"

"They're what you asked for to keep the Light Room clean," said Luke.

"Oh," said Ray, "Oh dear . . ." He was very disappointed.

"What's the matter?" asked Luke. "Were you expecting something else in the parcel?"

"Well," said Ray, "I just thought there might be . . . something . . . perhaps something a little bit exciting . . . I thought someone might just remember . . . what day it is."

"What day it is?" said Luke. "Why, it's Monday – the day I always come across to see you."

"I didn't mean Monday," said Ray. "I meant a special day . . . a special day for me . . . You see, it's . . . it's my birthday."

"Oh," said Luke, "Oh . . ." He was trying very hard not to smile because he knew something that Ray didn't know. Suddenly he grinned a great big grin into his beard.

"I think someone *has* remembered your birthday," he said. "Why don't you turn round and look over there?"

Ray spun round and gasped.
On the other side of the big
rock, a rowing-boat was tied
up. Four people stood there,

waving and shouting, "Happy
birthday, Ray!"

"Why, Auntie Milly," cried
Ray, "and Cousin Tim, and

Tom, and Tubby – what are you all doing here?"

"We rowed as quietly as we could, so we could creep up and surprise you while you were talking to Luke," laughed Cousin Tim.

"And look what we've brought you," said Tom.

"It's a yummy picnic," said Tubby.

They spread a white cloth on the ground and opened a huge picnic basket. Out came sausage rolls and sandwiches, crisps and biscuits, cheese and salad, chocolate fingers and

cake, apples and oranges, and
six bottles of lemonade.

"Oh me, oh my!" said Ray,

"what a wonderful picnic! I just don't know what to say."

"Let's sit down and tuck in," said Tubby.

"Come on, Luke," called Ray, "come and join us."

"Just a minute," called Luke, "there's something else for you here."

He carried three more parcels over from his boat – a big one, a small one and a smelly one wrapped in a paper bag.

Ray sniffed. "Phew," he said, "I'd better open this smelly parcel first. Why, it's fully of fishy snacks."

"That's the little tern's birthday picnic," said Luke.

"Zit, zit, zit," cried the little tern, swooping overhead.

"And what's in here?" asked Ray, opening the small parcel. "Why, it's full of meaty snacks."

"That's Croup's birthday picnic," said Luke.

"Croup, croup!" growled Croup greedily, and licked his lips.

"Now for the big parcel," said Ray, tearing off the paper. "I hope it's not more dusters and polish. Why, it's a cake, a very

tall cake, a lighthouse cake,
covered in red-and-white
icing!"

"That's for *your* birthday
picnic," said Luke.

"Oh me, oh my!" said Ray.

86

"What a cake, what a picnic, what a surprise!"

"You didn't think we'd all forget your birthday, did you?" asked Auntie Milly.

"Well," said Ray, "I knew *something* exciting was going to happen – I felt it in my bones – but I never expected this."

"That's enough talking," said Tubby. "Let's tuck in."

"Yes, let's," said Ray.

So for a while, you can guess, there wasn't any talking at all.

HANK PRANK AND HOT HENRIETTA
Jules Older

Hank and his hot-tempered sister, Henrietta, are always getting themselves into trouble but the doings of this terrible pair make for an entertaining series of adventures.

FIONA FINDS HER TONGUE
Diana Hendry

At home Fiona is a chatterbox, but whenever she goes out she just won't say a word. How she overcomes her shyness and 'finds her tongue' is told in this charming book.

NO PRIZE OR PRESENTS FOR SAM
Thelma Lambert

Two entertaining stories about Sam's ingenuity and determination.

THE TALE OF GREYFRIARS BOBBY
Virginia Derwent

A specially retold version for younger readers, of the true story of a scruffy Skye terrier who was faithful to his master even in death.

JOSH'S PANTHER

Fay Sampson

Josh never meant to deceive anyone about the paw print but his sister was such a clever know-all he just couldn't let her crow over him yet again.

CHRIS AND THE DRAGON

Fay Sampson

Chris just can't help getting into mischief – even when he decides to try extra hard to be good! Starting with an exploding dragon in a Christmas display and ending with another kind of dragon – Mrs Maltby the headmistress! – Chris's exploits around town and at school make hilarious reading.

THE SCHOOL POOL GANG

Geraldine Kaye

Billy is the head of the Black Lane Gang and he's always coming up with good ideas. So when money is needed for a new school pool, his first idea is to change the gang's name. His next idea – to raise money by giving donkey rides – leads to all sorts of unexpected and exciting happenings!

STICK TO IT, CHARLIE

Joy Allen

In these two 'Charlie' adventures, Charlie meets a new friend and finds a new interest – playing the piano. The new friend proves his worth when Charlie and the gang find themselves in a tight spot. As for the piano – well, even football comes second place!